Great Big Animals

GIANT GIRAFFES

By Ryan Nagelhout

Gareth Stevens
Publishing

Please visit our website, www.garethstevens.com. For a free color catalog of all our high-quality books, call toll free 1-800-542-2595 or fax 1-877-542-2596.

Library of Congress Cataloging-in-Publication Data

Giant giraffes / by Ryan Nagelhout.
    p. cm. — (Great big animals)
  Includes index.
ISBN 978-1-4339-9429-6 (pbk.)
ISBN   978-1-4339-9430-2 (6-Pack)
ISBN 978-1-4339-9428-9 (library binding)
1. Giraffe—Juvenile literature. I. Nagelhout, Ryan. II. Title.
QL737.U56 N34 2014
599.638—dc23

First Edition

Published in 2014 by
Gareth Stevens Publishing
111 East 14th Street, Suite 349
New York, NY 10003

Copyright © 2014 Gareth Stevens Publishing

Editor: Ryan Nagelhout
Designer: Sarah Liddell

Photo credits: Cover, p. 1 Mogens Trolle/Shutterstock.com; p. 5 Vadim Petrakov/Shutterstock.com; p. 7 Pichugin Dmitry/Shutterstock.com; p. 9 PRILL/Shutterstock.com; pp. 11, 24 (neck) Morkel Erasmus/Shutterstock.com; p. 13 Jonathan and Angela/Taxi/Getty Images; p. 15 Daleen Loest/Shutterstock.com; p. 17 Oleg Znamenskiy/ Shutterstock.com; p. 19 J Reineke/Shutterstock.com; pp. 21, 24 (spot) Tatiana Belova/Shutterstock.com; pp. 23, 24 (tongue) Szente A/Shutterstock.com.

Printed in the United States of America

CPSIA compliance information: Batch #CS13GS: For further information contact Gareth Stevens, New York, New York at 1-800-542-2595.

Contents

Giraffes are huge!

They are the tallest
animals on Earth.

The biggest are
19 feet tall.

They have very
long necks.

Their long legs make them run fast!

13

They love to eat leaves.

15

They go far
to find food.

They move in a group.
This is called a tower.

They have brown spots
on their fur.

21

Their tongues are
3 feet long!

23

Words to Know

neck

spot

tongue

Index

24